D0178075

For James the Cake
and for Mack ... our dog.

Gamesroom
ages 9 +

Bedroom
ages 6 – 9

Playroom
ages 4 – 7

Nursery
ages 1 – 4

Our Bloomsbury Book House
has a special room for each
age group –
this one is from the Nursery.

First published in Great Britain in 1995
Text and illustration copyright © 1995 Bernice Lum
The moral right of the author has been asserted.
Bloomsbury Publishing PLC, 2 Soho Square, London W1V 5DF
A CIP catalogue record for this book is available from The British Library
Manufactured in China

ISBN 0747520658

If I Had a Dog

Bernice Lum

Bloomsbury Children's Books

If I had a dog ...

I would call him Stanley

I would teach him to talk ...

and to read.

I would teach him to sing ...

and to dance.

and to skip ...

to use a knife and fork ...

and to make a cup of tea, h^ee h^ee.

I would teach him to juggle ...

and to balance things.

I would teach him to roller-skate ...

and even to ride a bicycle.

Most of all ...

I would teach him that I am his friend.